THE JADE HORSE
the Cricket and the Peach Stone

For Janice and Marilyn
—A. T.

For Alan, Linda, and all my family
—W. T.

Published by Caroline House
Boyds Mills Press, Inc.
A Highlights Company
815 Church Street
Honesdale, Pennsylvania 18431
Printed in Mexico

Publisher Cataloging-in-Publication Data
Tompert, Ann.
   The jade horse, the cricket, and the peach stone / by Ann Tompert ;
illustrated by Winson Trang.—1st ed.
[32]p. : col. ill. ; cm.
Summary : A boy overcomes a series of obstacles to bring a gift to the emperor
in this tale set in ancient China.
ISBN 1-56397-239-5
1. China—History—Juvenile fiction. [1. China—History—Fiction.]
I. Trang, Winson, ill. II. Title.
   [E]—dc20   1996   AC   CIP
Library of Congress Catalog Card Number 95-80782

First edition, 1996
Book designed by Tim Gillner
The text of this book is set in 14-point Zapf Calligraphy
The illustrations are done in acrylics

10 9 8 7 6 5 4 3 2 1

THE JADE HORSE
the Cricket and the Peach Stone

by Ann Tompert

Illustrated by Winson Trang

Boyds Mills Press

Long ago, in the year of the Horse, when Wu Ti was crowned emperor of the Middle Kingdom, every village in the country was expected to send him a gift. This caused great anxiety in Yang. The people of this small village were so poor that they had nothing of value to offer.

Then one day, Pan Su, a simple fisher-boy, snagged in his net a small horse carved from apple-green jade.

"You must take your jade horse to the emperor," the chief elder told Pan Su. "It will always remind him of this joyous year. And he will look kindly upon our village."

"But the journey is long," said Pan Su. "And I know nothing of things beyond our village."

"Do not be concerned," said the village astrologer. "The signs are good. You will have many trials, but all will end well. The gods have smiled on you."

"May it be as you say," Pan Su said.

Early the next morning, Pan Su set off on the three-day journey to the Great Jeweled Palace of Emperor Wu Ti. At nightfall he sought lodging at a wayside inn. There he fell in with a Cricket Master who had his champion, Dragon King, with him.

As he told tales of Dragon King's victories, the Cricket Master's snakelike eyes held Pan Su spellbound.

Afterward Pan Su showed him his jade horse.

"The emperor will be filled with joy whenever he looks upon it," said Pan Su.

The Cricket Master held the horse in his palm. His snakelike eyes glistened with greed. He leaned toward Pan Su. "But what if the emperor loses the jade horse, or it is stolen?" he hissed. "He'd be very angry, and he'd send his men to cut off your head."

"He wouldn't do that!" cried Pan Su. "Would he?"

The Cricket Master shrugged. "He might. Now if you had a champion cricket like Dragon King, things might be different."

"Do you really think so?" asked Pan Su.

"I've heard that the emperor desires champion crickets to add to his collection," said the Cricket Master. "Let us exchange my Dragon King for your jade horse."

Dozens of thoughts jumped around like grasshoppers in Pan Su's head as he looked from the jade horse to the cricket and back again.

"I think I'll keep the jade horse," he said at last.

And the Cricket Master flung it at him and stalked off.

The next morning, when Pan Su awoke, he found Dragon King beside him. His jade horse was gone. He complained to the innkeeper.

"The dimwit agreed to a trade," said the Cricket Master, shrugging his shoulders and winking at the innkeeper.

"That's not true!" protested Pan Su.

But the innkeeper hurried him on his way.

Dark thoughts of failure crept into Pan Su's head as he moved along the road. Even though Dragon King was a champion, he was only a cricket. Would he lose his head if he presented a lowly cricket to the great Wu Ti? To cheer himself up, he repeated over and over the promise of the village astrologer.

"All will end well. All will end well. All will end well."

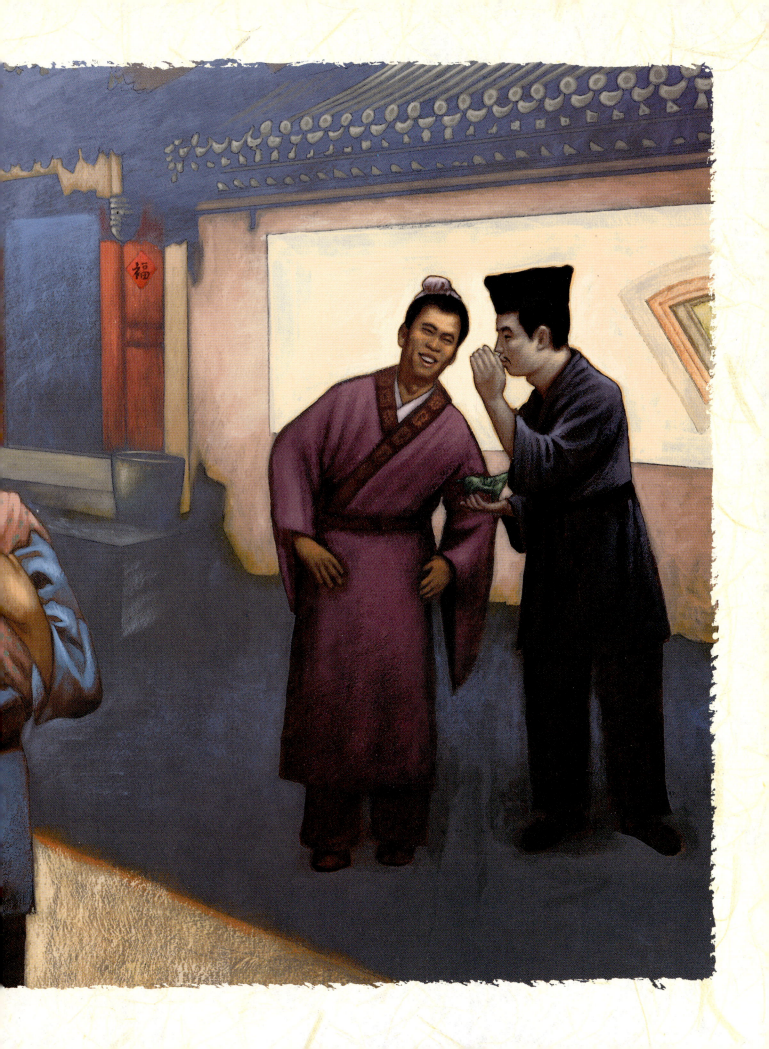

Nightfall found Pan Su at another wayside inn. Since several of the guests had their favorite crickets with them, the innkeeper brought out a fighting bowl.

When Pan Su was invited to put Dragon King into the fighting bowl, he refused. But the men goaded him until he agreed. And one by one Dragon King challenged and conquered the other crickets.

After the last match, a fat Salt Merchant, who had watched Dragon King with hungry eyes, insisted on treating Pan Su to tea and sesame cakes.

"Dragon King is just the cricket I need to round out my collection," he said. His puffy fingers toyed with the string of copper coins around his neck. "I can pay you well."

"I can't sell him," said Pan Su. "I'm carrying him to the Great Jeweled Palace. He'll bring joy to Emperor Wu Ti by winning fights."

"But what if he loses or is killed?" asked the merchant. "Crickets die every day. A dead cricket would not bring much joy to the emperor."

"That is so," agreed Pan Su, trying not to shudder at the thought of what might happen to his head.

"Salt is what you need," said the merchant. "The Emperor Wu Ti is very fond of roast suckling pig. And what is roast pig without salt to bring out its flavor?"

Pan Su nodded. "That is so."

But when the merchant offered to trade a bag of salt for Dragon King, Pan Su refused.

The next morning when he awoke, however, Pan Su found a bag of salt beside him instead of Dragon King. Remembering what had happened with the Cricket Master, he put the bag of salt in his sack and left the inn without complaining. Fears of failure again haunted him as he set out, but he pushed them aside.

"It will be as the astrologer promised," he told himself. "All will end well."

In the dawn's dim light, he had not noticed the small hole in his sack. As he trudged along, the hole grew bigger and bigger and the load on his back grew lighter and lighter.

"A burden always grows easier when the end of the journey is near," he thought.

At noon, Pan Su caught sight of the Great Jeweled Palace shimmering in the distance. He stopped to feast his eyes on its dazzling beauty. It was then that he discovered that his sack was empty. The salt was gone. He stood in the middle of the road, unaware of the crowds that swirled about him.

What was he to do? Where was he to go? For three days he had walked for nothing. All was not turning out well as the village astrologer had promised. He felt tears gathering in his eyes.

"You look like a heron who can't find the fish he thought he had speared," said a voice.

A white-bearded Scholar, stooped from years of bending over the books of ancient Chinese wisdom, stood beside him.

This small encouragement opened the floodgates. Out poured Pan Su's story of the jade horse, the cricket, and the bag of salt.

"I have nothing to give to the emperor," he said. "Now I will surely lose my head."

"Of course you won't," said the Scholar. "But you can give Emperor Wu Ti something he will prize above all other gifts. And all will end well as you were promised."

He handed Pan Su a peach.

"It's beautiful," said Pan Su, turning it about in his hands. "But how will it bring the emperor joy forever?"

He looked up.

The white-bearded Scholar had disappeared.

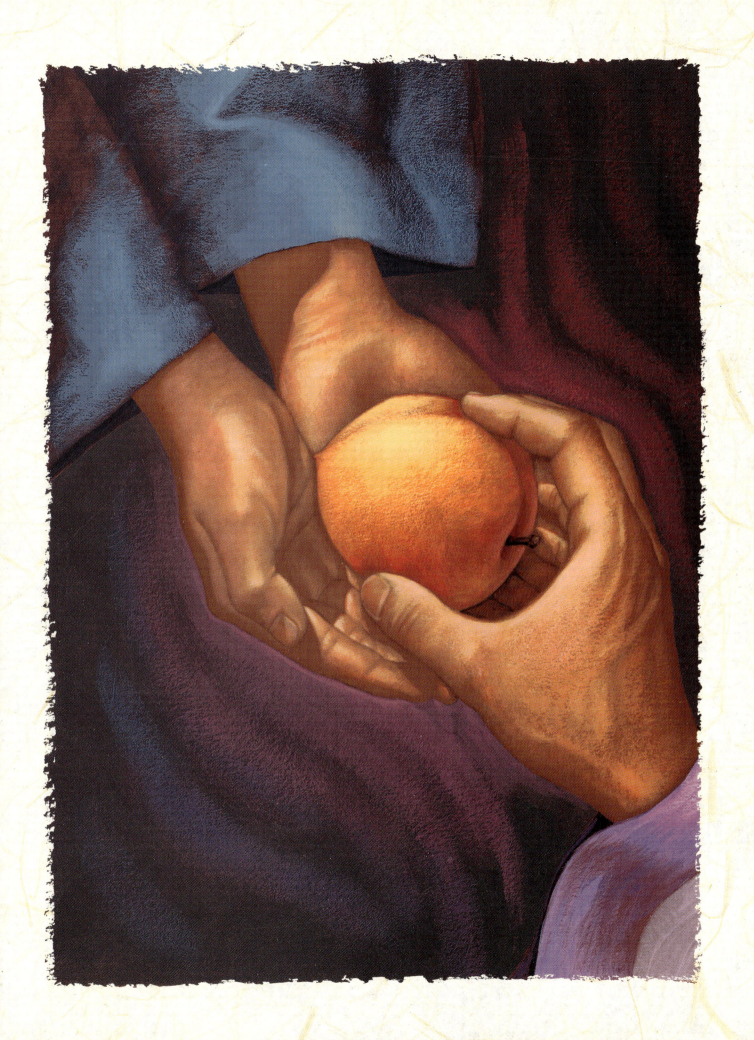

When he tried to find the Scholar to question him, Pan Su was swept along by the crowd of wayfarers who were hurrying toward the Great Jeweled Palace with their gifts.

Over the Jade Canal the crowd flowed, up Dragon Hill Head, and through a vast park dotted with lakes.

Pan Su was so dazzled by the sights that he almost forgot about his mission.

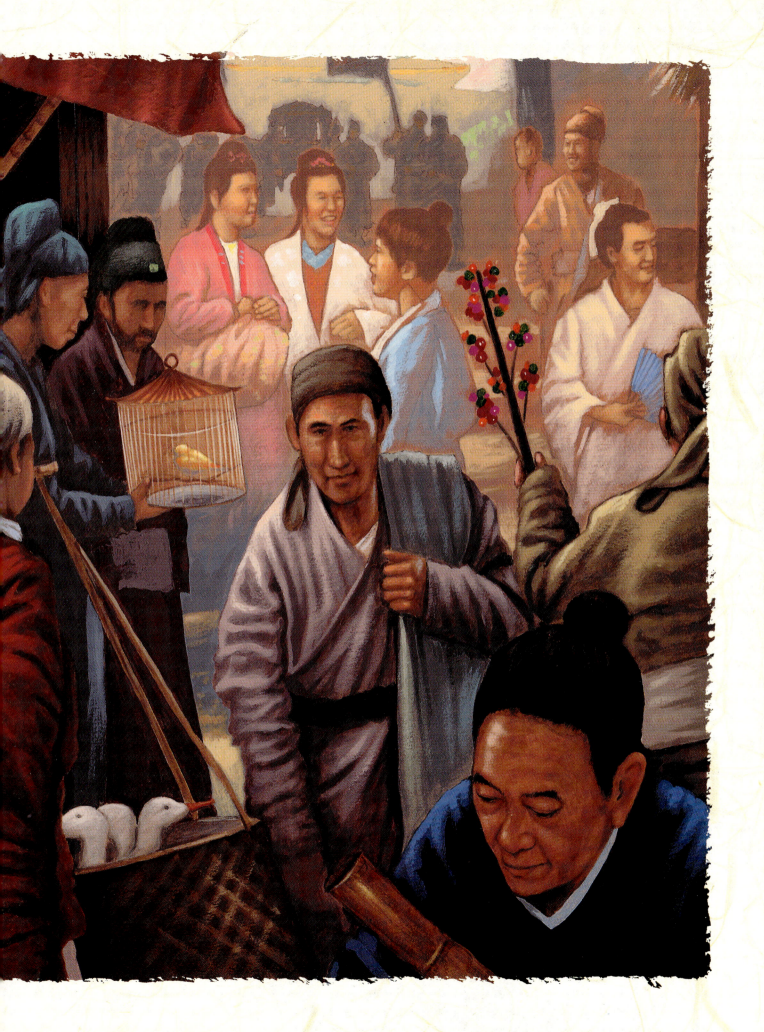

Pan Su was even more dazzled when he stepped into the Great Jeweled Palace and moved through one glittering room after another until he reached the Hall of the Silver Moon.

At one end of the hall sat the Emperor Wu Ti. Without knowing how, Pan Su found himself kneeling on a slab of marble and bowing nine times. On both sides, in front, and behind him, were countless others doing the same thing.

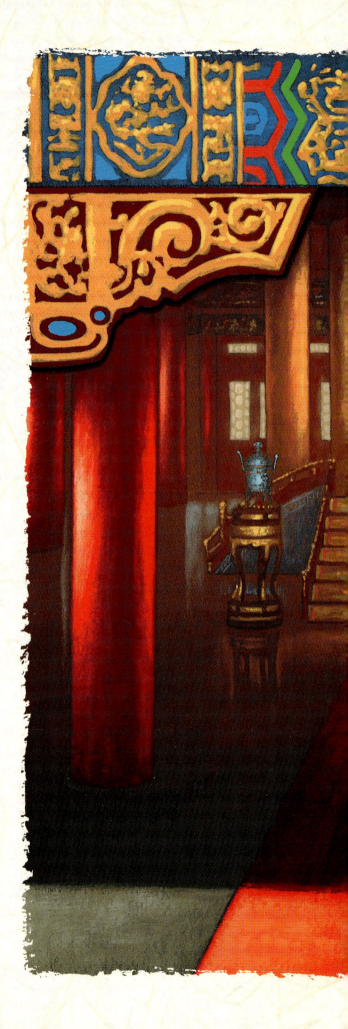

One by one, the gift-bearers offered their presents: jewel-embroidered robes, gilded shoes, rings and armlets studded with precious stones, and a multitude of other priceless things. Pan Su made himself as small as he could while the unsmiling emperor spurned one gift after another. His courage and his confidence in the peach slowly drained away until he felt like an empty shell. If only he could dry up completely and be blown away by a puff of wind.

Because he came from the smallest and poorest village, Pan Su was last.

"O most wise Son of the Sky," he began in a quaking voice, "the people of my village, Yang, beg you to look with favor upon this token of their homage. We hope it will bring you joy forever."

With trembling hands, he held out the peach.

A wave of gasps rippled around him. The stern-faced emperor signaled for silence and beckoned Pan Su to his throne. A frown creased the emperor's brow. He picked up his sword.

"Tell me," he demanded. "How is this peach different from the one I receive every year on my birthday?"

He glowered at Pan Su. Pan Su stared wide-eyed at the emperor's sword and cringed. He thought that surely he was about to lose his head.

"I don't know, Highness," he whispered. He could feel his eyes pricking with tears. How could he bear to fail after coming this far?

"Then how do you know it will bring me joy forever?" asked the emperor, testing the sword's edge with his finger.

"I know your first joy will come when you bite into the peach, Highness," said Pan Su.

The emperor chopped the air with his sword. "But my joy will be over after I eat this peach and throw away the stone."

"No! No!" cried Pan Su. "No one in my village, Yang, would throw it away. Plant the stone, Highness. And your second joy will come when the sprouts of a new tree appear."

A ghost of a smile drifted over the emperor's face. Pan Su could feel his confidence flow back, filling him with new life.

"And your third joy will be watching your tree grow until you can pick its first fruit. Then you can eat the peaches, plant the stones, grow more trees, and . . . "

"So on and so on and so on," said the emperor. He took the peach and, splitting it in two, gave half to Pan Su. Then the emperor closed his eyes and bit into his half. Pan Su held his breath. He might still lose his head if the taste did not please the emperor.

A blissful look crept over the emperor's face.

"Never have I tasted such a peach!" he declared. "Your gift truly will give me joy forever."

Pan Su drew a long sigh. All had ended well. He smiled to himself as he bit into his half of the peach.

DATE			